The Blue Ribbon Day

ALSO BY KATIE COURIC

The Brand New Kid

(Spanish title: *El Niño Nuevo*)

The Blue Ribbon Day

by
Katie Couric

Illustrated by
Marjorie Priceman

DOUBLEDAY
NEW YORK   LONDON   TORONTO   SYDNEY   AUCKLAND

To my mom and dad,

with love and gratitude

for helping me get through

all the bumps of childhood

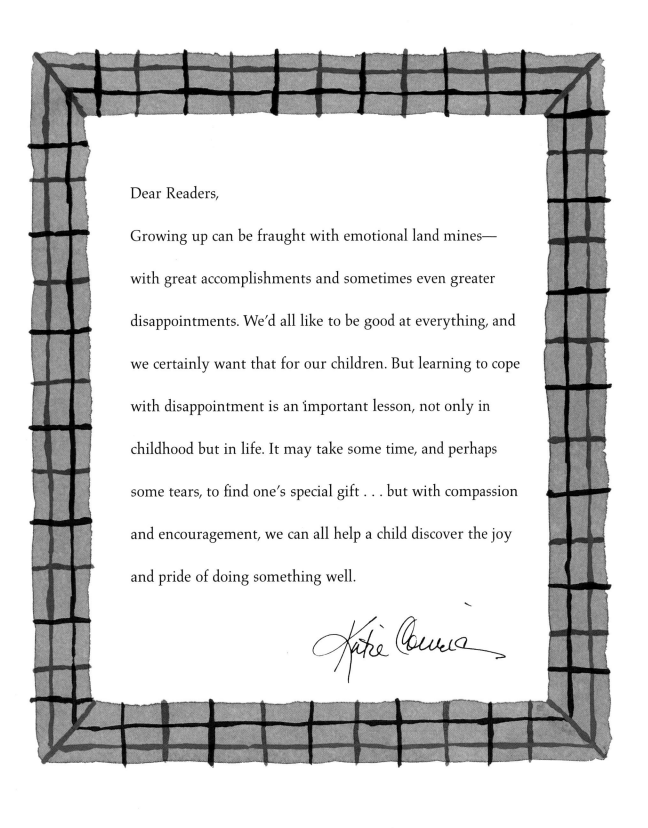

Dear Readers,

Growing up can be fraught with emotional land mines—with great accomplishments and sometimes even greater disappointments. We'd all like to be good at everything, and we certainly want that for our children. But learning to cope with disappointment is an important lesson, not only in childhood but in life. It may take some time, and perhaps some tears, to find one's special gift . . . but with compassion and encouragement, we can all help a child discover the joy and pride of doing something well.

Katie Couric

Ellie McSnelly and Carrie O'Toole
raced down the hall of Brookhaven School.
They stopped when they saw a big sign on the door
that read "TRYOUTS FOR SOCCER. TOMORROW AT FOUR."

Carrie said, "Great! Hey, let's give it a whirl!
I'd love to be known as a cool soccer girl!
Our skill and our speed are now terribly needed!
We'll beat 'em, we'll bust 'em, we'll be undefeated!"

Saturday came and the sky was bright blue;
Carrie hardly could wait to show what she could do.
When the clock struck 1:30 she screamed, "Mom, I'll see ya!
I'm heading to tryouts to be the next Mia!"

She got there and saw Ellie running so fast,
her ponytail waving at the girls as she passed.

"Over here! Over here!" Ellie heard Carrie shout.
Carrie ran up to kick but instead she wiped out.

She watched Patty Smiley moving downfield,
passing to Ellie with grace and with zeal.
Ellie dribbled and passed, wow, was she on a roll.
Then she got the ball back and she kicked in a goal!

And so practice went for the rest of the hour.
Ellie said, "That was fun, but I sure need a shower!"
Carrie said, "When it comes to this game, El, you rule!
I'll see you on Monday," and Ellie said, "Cool!"

Carrie was glad she'd gone out on a limb,
til she saw the big sign hanging up in the gym:
"THE FOLLOWING GIRLS COME TO SATURDAY'S GAME."
Carrie looked and she looked but could not find her name.

She watched some of the girls who were jumping for joy;
they were hugging and screaming and shouting oh boy!
Ellie said, "Hey there, Carrie, can't wait til we play,"
but with tears in her eyes, Carrie just walked away.

Ellie followed her out and said, "Please, Carrie, wait!
You should be on the team, I think you played great!"
Carrie said, "Thank you, Ellie, that's really so sweet,
but I'm no good at soccer. I've got two left feet."

When Carrie got home she was feeling so blue,
she cried to her mom and said, "What will I do?"
Her mom said, "Don't worry, I know you are sad,
but you couldn't feel good if you never felt bad."

She hugged Carrie and said, "Honey, give it some time.
We're all good at something, you'll have your chance to shine.
Everybody's a star, a brilliant creation,
the trouble is finding the right constellation!"

Carrie thought that she'd try to take those words to heart.
The next day she was ready to make a new start,
and it turned out that she'd picked a very good day—
the school science fair was just one week away!

Her lab partner, Lazlo, said, "Let's have some fun.
You've always said two heads are better than one."
Carrie took just a minute to think it all through,
and said, "There IS a project I've been wanting to do."

So the two got together that day after school.
With Miss Rigg's supervision (you know, that's the rule),
they got out their beakers and their Bunsen burners
and decided to find out if they were fast learners.

They boiled beakers of water, then lowered the heat;
they added some sugar to make it so sweet;
they filled them and filled them til they couldn't add more;
and transferred the liquid with a slow, steady pour.

They added food coloring to give it some flair,
then put Popsicle sticks in the cups with great care.
Then they waited a week to see what would appear.
Could they enter this project? It soon would be clear.

It worked! They'd made crystals! All colors and sizes,
a mobile of crystalline sugar surprises!
Not cubes, but all oblongs with slants on the ends,
and they watched as they glistened, these two special friends.

They submitted their project, one of twenty-three,
and the next day the whole school was invited to see
all the budding young scientists and what they could do,
and on Carrie and Lazlo's was a ribbon so blue!

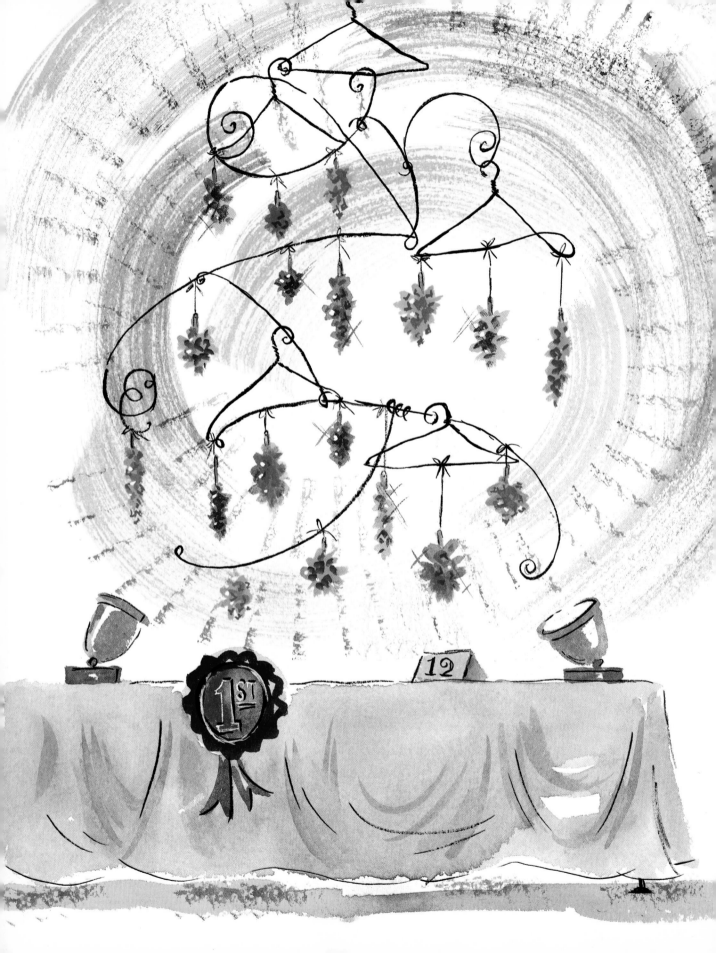

They did it! First place in the school science fair!
They screamed and they hugged and they jumped in the air.
Ellie ran up and high-fived them and said, "I'm so proud
to know two budding Einsteins!" And they all laughed out loud.

The next day, it was Carrie who was feeling so proud
as she stood in the midst of a big, cheering crowd.
And from way down the block you could hear Carrie roar
when El made a goal and they won! 5 to 4!

Published by Doubleday
a division of Random House, Inc.

Doubleday and the portrayal of an anchor with a dolphin are trademarks of
Random House, Inc.

Library of Congress Cataloging-in-Publication Data

Couric, Katie, 1957–
The blue ribbon day / by Katie Couric ; illustrated by Marjorie
Priceman.—1st ed.
p. cm.
Summary: When Carrie is disappointed not to make the school soccer team,
she turns her attention to creating a science fair project.
[1. Self-esteem—Fiction. 2. Self-perception—Fiction. 3. Soccer—Fiction.
4. Science projects—Fiction. 5. Schools—Fiction. 6. Stories in rhyme.]
I. Priceman, Marjorie, ill. II. Title.

PZ8.3.C88332B1 2004

[E]—dc22   2003068829

ISBN 0-385-50142-0

PRINTED IN THE UNITED STATES OF AMERICA

October 2004
First Edition
3   5   7   9   10   8   6   4   2

```
              HOAKX   +
                      E
                      COURI


COURIC, KATIE
     THE BLUE RIBBON DAY

08/05
```